Gracie

by Robin Ballard

Greenwillow Books, New York

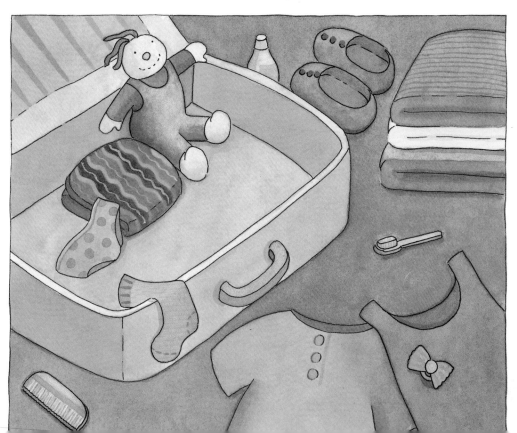

For my parents

Pen and ink and watercolors were used for
the full-color art.
The text type is Folio Light.

Printed in Singapore by Tien Wah Press
First Edition
10 9 8 7 6 5 4 3 2 1

Library of Congress Cataloging-in-Publication Data

Ballard, Robin.
  Gracie / by Robin Ballard.
      p.   cm.
  Summary: Gracie describes life in her two separate
homes, one with her mother and one with her father.
  ISBN 0-688-11806-2.
  ISBN 0-688-11807-0 (lib. bdg.)
  [1. Divorce—Fiction.
2. Mothers and daughters—Fiction.
3. Fathers and daughters—Fiction.]
I. Title. PZ7.B2125Gp   1993
[E]—dc20   92-14245   CIP   AC

I have a mama and a papa, then there is me, Gracie.
Some parents live together, but mine live apart.

Mama's house is at the bottom of the mountains,

and Papa's house is at the sandy beach.

When I am with Papa, we feed the seagulls
bits of cinnamon toast. And at low tide
I can hold a starfish in my hand.

We peddle our bikes to the end of
the pier so we can whale watch.
Or if the ocean is not too rough,
we walk into its waves.

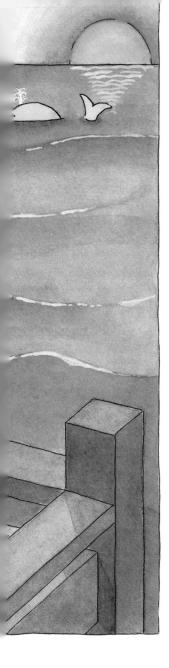

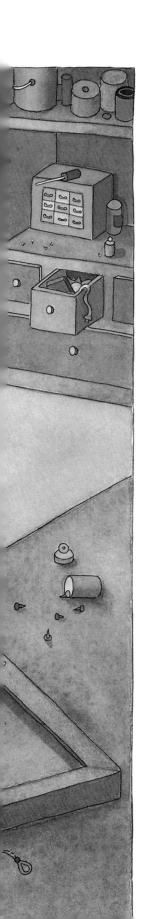

While Papa builds things
out of wood, I build
things out of sand.
I found a beautiful shell.
I know Mama will like it.

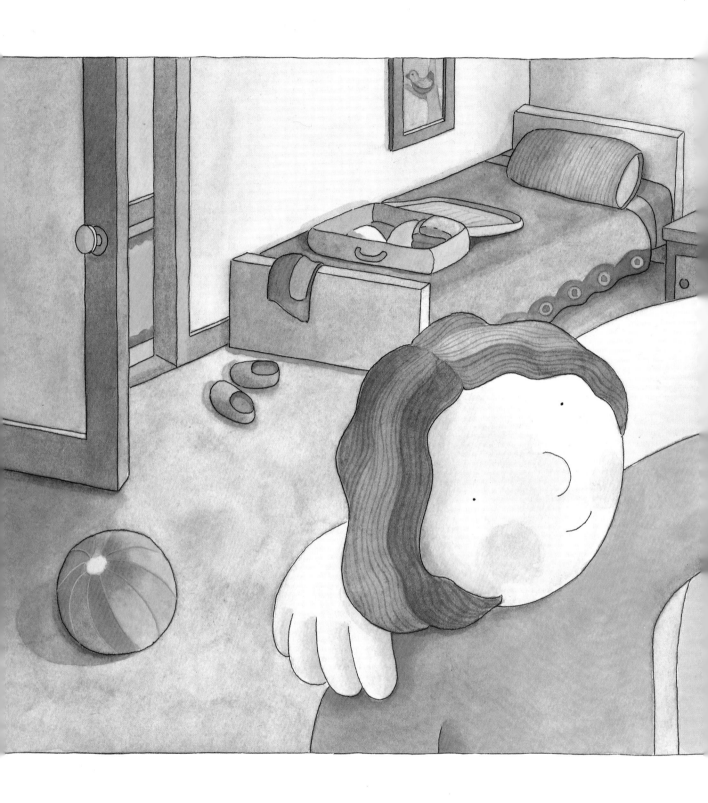

We are very quiet when it's time to say good-bye.

Papa says he will miss me. I will miss him, too.

I wonder what it was like when
my parents were together.

They said they were happy, and then
they were not. But all that
happened before I can remember.

Mama is happy when she sees me coming.

We jump around and talk a lot. I am happy, too.

There is a path that we climb to
where the huckleberries grow.
We pick just enough to make a pie.

When we go fishing in our silver-colored boat, we sing the fish a song.

Or if it's not too cold,

we go swimming off the dock.

Our backyard is one
big garden that we
planted from tiny seeds.
I am drawing a picture
of it for Papa.

I live with my Mama, and I live with my Papa.
I have two places that are home for me.